MY
GRANDMOTHER'S
CLOCK

For Jay, G.M.

To Sarah, Nancy and Jack,
with love, S.L.

First published in hardback in Great Britain by HarperCollins Publishers Ltd in 2002
First published in paperback by Collins Picture Books in 2003

1 3 5 7 9 10 8 6 4 2

ISBN: 0 00 710652 1

Collins Picture Books is an imprint of the Children's Division,
part of HarperCollins Publishers Ltd.

Text copyright © Geraldine McCaughrean 2002
Illustrations copyright © Stephen Lambert 2002

The author and illustrator assert the moral right to be identified
as the author and illustrator of the work.
A CIP catalogue record for this title is available from the British Library.

The HarperCollins website address is: www.**fire**and**water**.com

Printed in Hong Kong

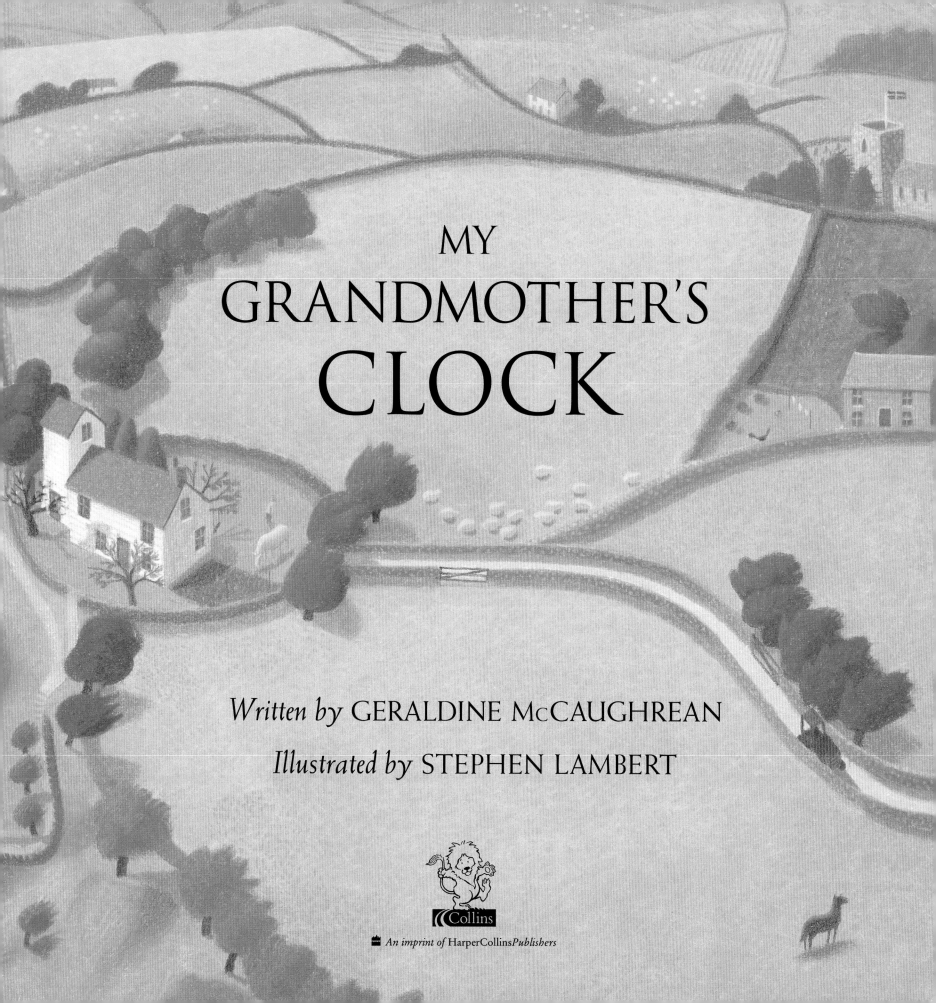

MY GRANDMOTHER'S CLOCK

Written by GERALDINE McCAUGHREAN

Illustrated by STEPHEN LAMBERT

Collins

An imprint of HarperCollinsPublishers

In my grandmother's house there is
a grandfather clock, but it does not go.
The hands on its big face never move.
Once, I opened the door in the
front of the clock to find out why,
and there was nothing inside
but one umbrella,
a walking stick
and a picture of King Zog.

You should get the clock mended, I said.

Why? said Grandad. Twice a day it tells the right time!

Why, said Grandma, when I have so many
other clocks telling me the time?

I looked around me.
There are no other clocks in
my grandmother's house.
Where? I asked.

Grandma said, I can count seconds by the beating
of my heart. Have you noticed how the seconds
go much quicker when life is exciting?

Moments are much shorter than seconds.
They are gone in the blink of an eye.

A minute is how long it takes to
think a thought and put it into words.
In two, I can read a page of my book.

An hour is the time it takes
for the bathwater to go cold…
or for your grandfather to
read the newspaper…

...or both of us to walk the dog.

I can judge the age of the morning by
the shadows shortening under the magnolia tree.
By the time the shadows are long again,
the day is nearly full-grown.

Each morning, the birds wake me
with their early morning call.

Every evening, I look out of the window
and the lights in the other houses
are signalling to the ships at sea:
winking on, time for supper
winking off, time for bed.

You know each day is over, don't you,
when your mother kisses you goodnight.

But how do you tell the days of the week? I asked my grandmother.

That's easy, too, she said.
Monday by the smell of baking
curling from the open windows…

Tuesday by the trawlers
coming home…

Wednesday by the dustmen
banging on the bins…

Thursday by the scuffs on the school shoes…

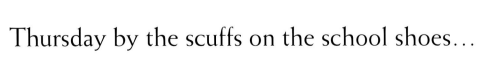

and Friday by the greyness
in the faces on the train.

I can tell when the week ends,
because things slow down.
On Saturdays there is time to play.

And on Sundays, families
like ours get together.
(That's why I like Sundays best.)

In one week, enough dust settles
on the grandfather clock for it to
need dusting.

In one month, the moon waxes and wanes,
night weaving its golden chrysalis, then
gradually hatching out into darkness.

The tides tell time, too. They keep Moon Time.

The seasons are easy, of course:
what with the blossom in
the spring,

the heat-hazy-waves in summer,

the autumn trees on fire,

and the frost-fringed days
when your breath turns
to dragon smoke.

As for the years, said my grandmother sadly,

you can count them easily in the number

of my grey hairs and the lines in my face.

And how much closer your head comes to mine.

A lifetime, of course, you

can measure in all kinds of ways:

in birthdays

in friends

in what you own…

or in what you remember.

But when you are lucky enough, like us,

and have a grandchild, you know

that Time has come full circle.

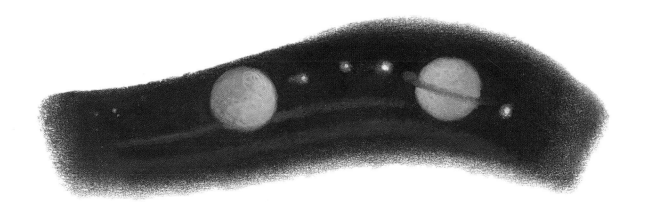

And as for the centuries, well, we have the
comets in their ellipses, the sun and moon's eclipses.
The whole universe, you see, is wound up like a clock.
And then there are the stars!

My grandmother closed her eyes, but it was for
more than a moment, so she wasn't blinking.

Well, the stars tell us that Time's just
too big to fit inside any watch or clock
– even the one in the hall.

But you still need your grandfather clock, I told my grandmother.

She sighed patiently. And why is that?

Well, I said…

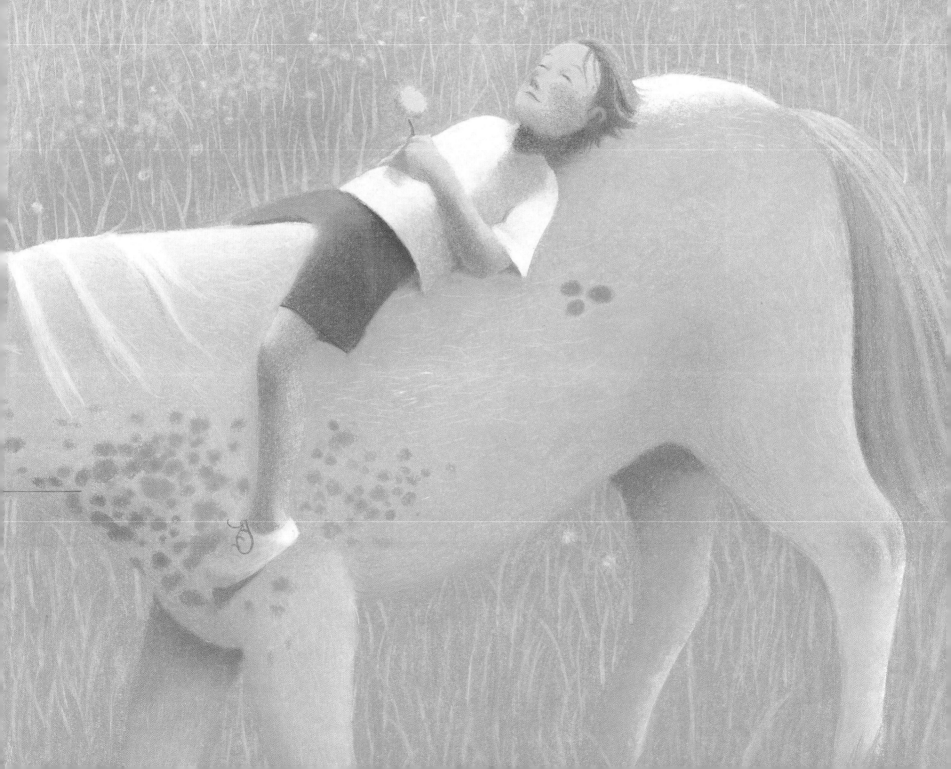

Where else would
you keep your
umbrella and
Grandpa's
walking stick
and the picture of
King Zog?